This Little Tiger book
belongs to:

_____

_____

_____

For my family, for always being behind me xxx
-EY

For Scarlet, Gabby, Elliott and Annie, love you from the bottom of my heart x
-SS

LITTLE TIGER PRESS
1 The Coda Centre, 189 Munster Road,
London SW6 6AW
www.littletiger.co.uk
First published in Great Britain 2013
This edition published 2013

Text copyright © Steve Smallman 2013
Illustrations copyright © Emma Yarlett 2013
Steve Smallman and Emma Yarlett have asserted their
rights to be identified as the author and illustrator of this
work under the Copyright, Designs and Patents Act, 1988
A CIP catalogue record for this book is available from the
British Library
All rights reserved • ISBN 978-1-84895-586-8
Printed in China • LTP/1400/0552/0313
10 9 8 7 6 5 4 3 2 1

SQUIRREL'S
B'DAY
BASH

Friday

Bear's Big Bottom

STEVE SMALLMAN

EMMA YARLETT

LITTLE TIGER PRESS
London

Bear was friendly,
Bear was sweet,

The nicest bear
you'd ever meet,

With little paws and little feet...

AAAA ARGHHH

...And a very BIG bear bottom!

His best friends really didn't mind
That Bear had such a big behind,
It made him easier to find –
You can't hide Bear's BIG bottom!

But when they tried to watch TV
Bear's bottom filled the whole settee!
And no one could sit comfortably,
Because of Bear's big bottom.

The pool was emptied with one splash!
Because of Bear's big bottom.

When Hedgehog fetched
the birthday cake,

Which everyone
had helped to make,

Bear made a really
BIG mistake –

He squashed it with
his bottom!

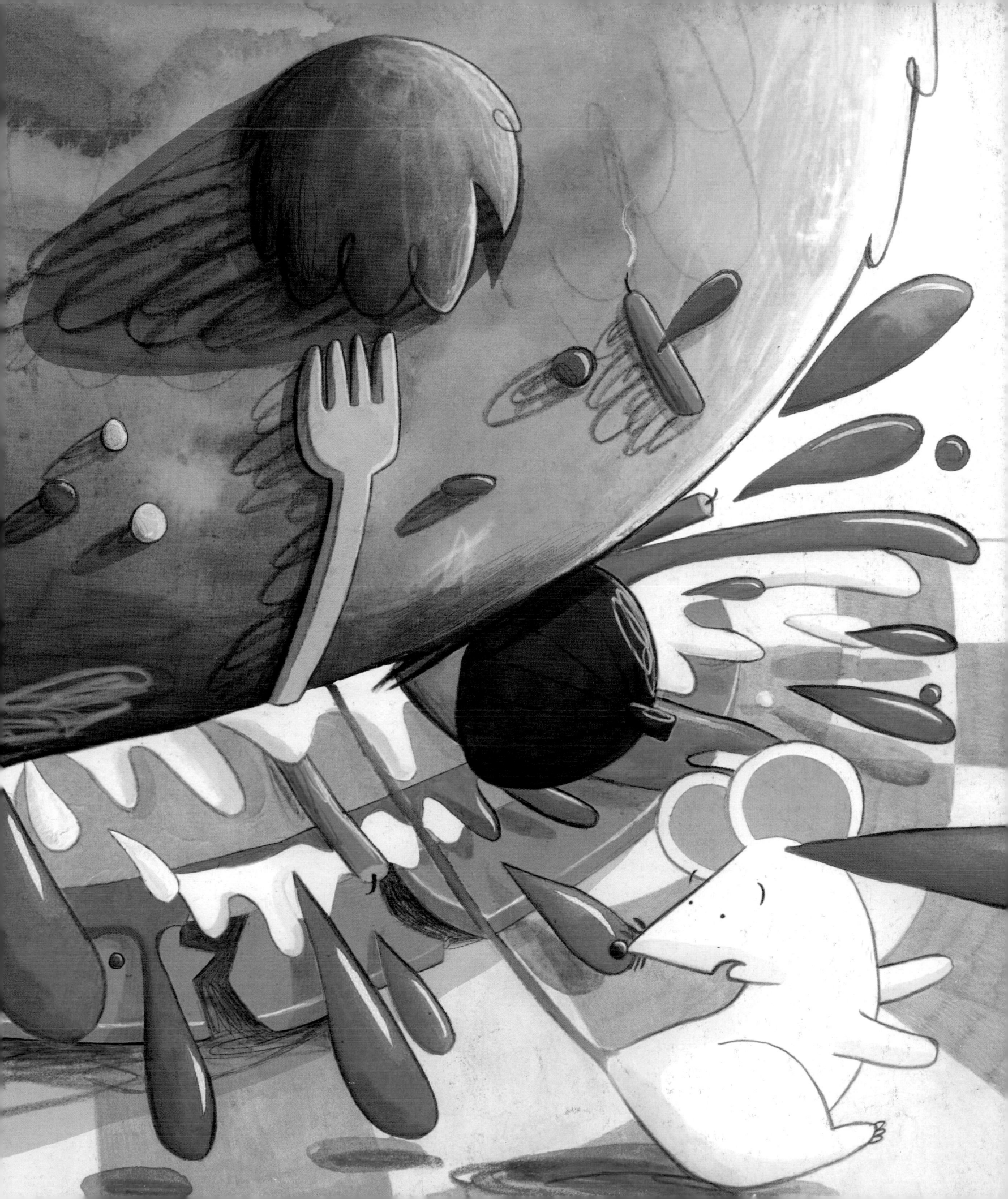

"You've spoiled our day!"
Bear's friends all cried,
And poor Bear felt so sad inside,
He ran away and tried to hide
His clumsy, big bear bottom.

The friends set off to search for Bear,

They shouted,
" Bear are you in there ? "

But then they
got a nasty scare . . .

...FOX tried to bite their bottoms!

"Quick, help us, Bear!"
they cried in fear,

SNAP
SNAP

Bear shouted right back, loud and clear,
"I'm trying but I'm stuck in here,
Because of my BIG bottom!"

Bear's little friends
began to feel
They'd soon be Fox's
evening meal!

But then Fox gave a scaredy squeal
And fell back on HIS bottom!
"A Monster!"
yelled the fox and fled.

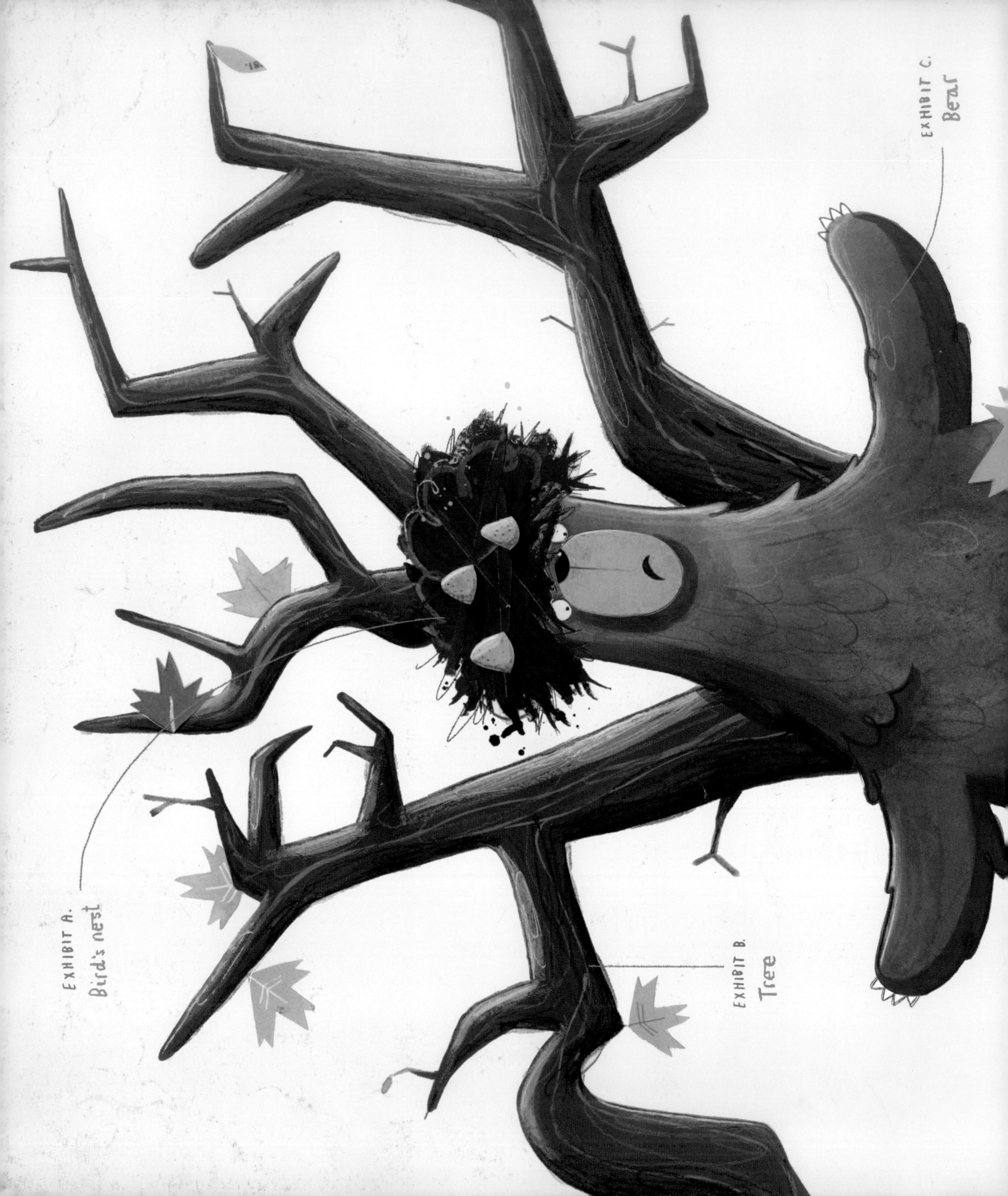

EXHIBIT C.
Bear

EXHIBIT A.
Bird's nest

EXHIBIT B.
Tree

"It's only me!" Bear softly said.
"I've got a bird's nest on my head
And a tree stuck to my bottom."

They helped Bear get his bottom free,
And then he took them home for tea,
And everyone cheered happily,
"HOORAY for Bear's
BIG BOTTOM!"